It Zwibble *and the*
Greatest Cleanup Ever!

Created by
WereRoss and WerEnko

Written by Lisa V. Werenko

Illustrated by Tom Ross

SCHOLASTIC INC.

New York   Toronto   London   Auckland   Sydney

Dedicated with love to our very BIG and very UNUSUAL families

ISBN 0-590-44840-4

12 11 10 9 8 7 6 5 4 3 2 1   1 2 3 4 5 6/9

Printed in the U.S.A.   24

First Scholastic printing, April 1991

In the Buzzville Forest on the top of a purple
hill lives a very BIG and very UNUSUAL family.

There's a magical dinosaur fairy named It Zwibble, some forest friends, and a lot of star-tailed dinosaurs called the Zwibble Dibbles.

One evening the Zwibble Dibble family was busy doing the kinds of things they like to do after a day at the mill. It Zwibble and some of the Zwibble Dibbles were up on the roof watching for falling stars.

Fred the Moose was in the nursery singing a tender lullaby to a few of the littlest ones.

DIPPER

Tu the Toucan was showing the plans for his latest invention to Craighead the skeptical Shrew. Craighead took one look at Tu's plans and snickered. "I've been waiting to see this dream car of yours forever. You'll never get the parts you need!"

Suddenly the quiet time at the mill was interrupted by a loud shout coming from the back porch. "I got it, by golly!" Grampa Cobb called out excitedly. "It's called Sycamore and Pond. I just remembered how to get there!"
Everyone hurried to the back porch to hear what all the excitement was about.

Grampa smiled as he told the family about a beautiful spot where he used to picnic and swim as a young beaver. The spot was cool and shaded by trees. The pond was filled with clear, blue water. It sounded so wonderful the whole family wanted to go right away! But it was almost bedtime. It Zwibble wisely decided that it would be best to start fresh in the morning. All that night the Zwibble Dibbles were so excited they could hardly sleep!

BUZZVILLE
FOREST
MAP

Bright and early the next morning, the whole family started off
on their hike to Sycamore and Pond. Everyone was very excited.
They couldn't wait to see the most beautiful place in the
world! It was a long, long walk. The littlest ones had to
be carried. "Hey, Tu, where's that dream car we've been
waiting for?" teased Craighead the Shrew. Finally after
a lot of uphills and downs, they rounded the bend
and arrived at Sycamore and Pond.

But it wasn't beautiful at all! It was littered with trash and ruined by garbage. "Oh, no!" said Fred. "We can't picnic here!"
"It was once so lovely," Grampa sighed.
"Let's go home," said the Zwibble Dibbles.

But It Zwibble had a better idea. "I'll bet if we work together we can make this place beautiful again," he said. "And then we can picnic and swim."

"It's a big job," said Grampa.

"Too big!" grumbled the Shrew.

But the Zwibble Dibbles wanted to try. It Zwibble explained to the Shrew that the cleanup would go a lot faster if the whole family pitched in. And it sure did! Before the day was through, they had collected 864 bags of garbage! "Now all we have to do is take it to the dump," said It Zwibble.

But when they reached the dump it was closed. There was no room for any more garbage. The dump was too full with plastics and Styrofoam—things that won't break down in the soil. "What will we do with all of the garbage?" the Zwibble Dibbles asked. "We can't leave it here, and we can't put it back in the woods."

So they carried all 864 bags of garbage back to the mill.
"We'll never picnic and swim," complained the Shrew.
"It isn't our garbage! Why should we have to take care of it?"
"I know it isn't fair," said It Zwibble kindly. "But it is our
earth, and the earth needs us all to help."

"I think the best garbage would be no garbage," Fred said.
"If only there were a way to get rid of all the garbage," sighed Grampa.
"It's no use!" grumbled the Shrew. "All that time we spent cleaning, all the effort, it's all useless—just like that garbage out there. Useless!"

"That's it, Craighead!" shouted It Zwibble. "What a great idea!"
"What idea are you talking about?" Fred asked.
"Right now the garbage out there is useless," It Zwibble explained.
"But if we can find ways to reuse it all we'll have no garbage. Then we can picnic and swim!"

The next morning everyone got to work separating the garbage into different piles—glass, metal, and paper. Then they put their heads together to find ways to reuse or recycle everything.

"What if we find something we don't know what to do with?" asked the Shrew.

"Well, if that happens," It Zwibble answered, "just put it to the side." Cobb helped the Zwibble Dibbles find new uses for all the paper.

It Zwibble helped the Zwibble Dibbles recycle the old bottles. They stored enough lemonade to last for three summers!

I DON'T KNOW WHAT TO DO WITH IT PILE

LEMONADE

All the old fruits and vegetables were added to the compost pile.
"That will help our flowers grow!" said Fred.

The old tin cans were perfect for potting all the geraniums. After a lot of work and fun, the paper, glass, tin cans, old vegetables and fruits—everything—was recycled.

"Yip! Yip! Yippee! We did it!" shouted the Zwibble Dibbles. "Now we can picnic and swim!"

But the Zwibble Dibbles had cheered too soon. All of a sudden they looked and saw that their work wasn't done at all! Everyone had been so busy working that no one had noticed that the I-Don't-Know-What-to-Do-With-It Pile had really grown.

"Oh, nothing's fair!" whined the Shrew. "Nothing works out! We're always waiting! Waiting to swim! Waiting to picnic! Waiting for Tu's silly old dream car. Who cares about Sycamore and Pond? It's too far away, anyway!"

"Hey, Shrew," Tu smiled. "I think you just gave us *another* great idea!"

Now Tu knew just what to do with the
leftover garbage. He shared his idea with his
friends. They all stayed up into the night.

In the morning
the Zwibble Dibble family
headed off for Sycamore and Pond
in the most incredible, pedal-powered, non-polluting
jalopy ever seen!

"Just as I remembered it," Grampa Cobb said.
"It was worth waiting for," said It Zwibble.

They stayed all day.

Until the stars came out.